There's a
HUMMINGBIRD

in My
BACKYARD

GARY BOGUE

ILLUSTRATED BY CHUCK TODD

There's a
HUMMINGBIRD
in My
BACKYARD

Heyday Books, Berkeley, California

Heyday Books, founded in 1974, works to deepen people's understanding and appreciation of the cultural, artistic, historic, and natural resources of California and the American West. It operates under a 501(c)(3) nonprofit educational organization (Heyday Institute) and, in addition to publishing books, sponsors a wide range of programs, outreach, and events.

To help support Heyday or to learn more about us, visit our website at www.heydaybooks. com, or write to us at P.O. Box 9145, Berkeley, CA 94709.

Library of Congress Cataloging-in-Publication Data

Bogue, Gary.
  There's a hummingbird in my backyard /
Gary Bogue; illustrated by Chuck Todd.
     p. cm.
  Summary: In their own backyard, the Baker
family observes a pair of hummingbirds from their
courtship dance through the day the fledglings are
ready to leave the nest and return on their own.
Includes facts about hummingbirds, and related
websites and books.
  Includes bibliographical references.
  ISBN 978-1-59714-131-4 (hardcover : alk. paper)
  1. Hummingbirds--Juvenile fiction. [1. Hummingbirds--Fiction.] I. Todd, Chuck, ill. II.
Title. III. Title: There is a hummingbird in my backyard.
  PZ10.3.B6372Tgt 2010
  [E]--dc22   2009037465

Book design by Lorraine Rath

Orders, inquiries, and correspondence should be addressed to:
     Heyday Books
     P. O. Box 9145, Berkeley, CA 94709
     (510) 549-3564, Fax (510) 549-1889
     www.heydaybooks.com

Printed in China by O.G. Printing Productions, Ltd.
Manufactured in March 2010

10   9 8 7 6 5 4 3 2 1

For Lois, because she's best!
—*Gary Bogue*

For Anita, Sheridan, and Sienna
and with thanks to Jeff
—*Chuck Todd*

The Baker family—Mom, Dad, and Kelly—are in their backyard playing ball with their dog, Digger. They don't see the Anna's hummingbird that is watching them from her perch on a slender branch.

Hummingbirds are so tiny you hardly ever notice them when they sit still.

"Hummers" have to be very careful where they build their nests, because jays, snakes, and cats would like to eat their babies.

Mama hummer might put her nest on the very end of a slender branch that bobs up and down in the wind. A jay would have trouble landing on that branch.

She might hide her nest in a hanging plant on the back patio. The nest would be hard for a jay to find.

She might put the nest on top of a wind chime. That would be too high for a cat or a snake to climb, and close enough to people to frighten a jay away.

Dad and Kelly see two hummingbirds zooming around the yard. "Dad! Look! What are those little birds doing?"

"I think they're male and female hummingbirds," says Dad. "He's doing all that fancy flying to catch her eye and show her what strong babies they could have. After they breed, she will build a nest, lay two eggs, and raise her babies by herself. Hummingbird dads really have it easy!"

"Can we buy a hummingbird feeder, dad?" asks Kelly. "We could help feed them, and watch them when they come to eat!"

Did you ever wonder what hummingbirds use to build their nests?

Hummingbirds fill their nests with fairytale fillings. They use lichens, dried moss, dried grass, spiderwebs gathered from trees, and soft feathers plucked from their own bodies.

CHUCK TODD

The mama hummer might
even snatch a fuzzy beakful of
loose hair from Digger while
he's taking a nap.

One day when Dad and Kelly are out watering and raking their flower garden, Mama hummingbird suddenly swoops down into the middle of the spray from Dad's hose.

"Why doesn't she use a bird bath?" Kelly wonders.

"I suspect that little birds that spend most of their lives in the air prefer showers to baths," laughs Dad.

Mama hummingbird sits on her nest day and night to keep the eggs warm while the two babies are growing inside. She only leaves for a few minutes at a time to find something to eat. The shape of the nest and the soft feathers inside keep the eggs warm and safe until she gets back.

Sixteen days after the mama hummingbird lays her eggs, they hatch. She has two babies! Because their beaks are very short, it is easy for mama to feed them. By the time the babies are ready to leave the nest, their beaks will have grown very long.

What does a mama hummingbird feed her tiny babies?

She snatches flying insects, like mosquitoes and fruit flies, right out of the air.

She grabs tasty spiders from their webs in trees and on the walls of the house.

She collects sweet nectar from flowers in the garden, and sugar water from the hummingbird feeder.

"I've been reading about hummingbirds," says Dad. "Did you know that the Aztecs used to decorate their ceremonial cloaks with hummingbird feathers? Would you like to have a hummingbird feather coat?"

Kelly shakes her head no. "Nope! I think the feathers look lots better on the hummingbirds!"

Hummingbirds see reddish colors best. That means they like to drink from red, purple, orange, violet, and pink flowers.

CHUCK TODD

Because hummingbirds are always zooming around the sky, they burn up a lot of energy. They really need a lot of food.

Male hummers chase the other hummingbirds away from their territory so they'll always have enough food for themselves.

There are plenty of flowers and insects to go around. The hummers that get chased away will still be able to find something to eat.

During nesting season, the male hummingbird isn't always so grumpy. He lets the mama hummingbird eat anything she wants in "his" yard, because she has to feed her babies.

How to use hummingbird feeders in your own yard: Mix 1 part granulated sugar to 4 parts water. This mix tastes about the same as real flower nectar. It also has about the same amount of energy for the hungry hummers.

There are many different kinds of hummingbird feeders. Pick one you like, the hummingbird doesn't care. Feeders are usually red because hummingbirds like to eat from flowers that are red (remember?).

Be sure to keep the feeder clean and the food fresh.

Hang your feeder about 5 to 6 feet off the ground, in a spot where you can watch it from a window. Keep it out of the sun so the nectar doesn't get too hot and burn a hummingbird's beak.

If you plant flowers that hummingbirds like to drink from in your yard, a tiny bird will soon stop by for a visit.

Just 18 to 23 days after they hatch, the baby hummers will be ready to leave the nest and learn about the big world around them.

It's a big, wide, dangerous world out there for baby hummingbirds. They have to watch out for jays, cats, and maybe even a hungry praying mantis.

Oh no! Sometimes it can be dangerous even while they are still living in their nest!

"Mommy! Daddy! The babies are gone!"

Two days later, Kelly is watering the flowers in the backyard, hoping the babies were big enough to get away.

"Mom, Dad! Come see this! They just came back! They're all okay! The babies and the mama are okay!"

A FEW WORDS ABOUT HUMMINGBIRDS

Hummingbirds are the tiniest birds there are.

Hummingbirds are found only in the Americas (Western Hemisphere).

There are more kinds of hummingbirds than any other bird in the world. The Anna's hummers in our little story are just one of 343 species.

A hummingbird's heart beats 1,260 times per minute. They have the fastest wing beats of any bird.

Hummingbirds can migrate great distances—2,000 miles from Canada to Panama, and that includes 500 miles nonstop over the Gulf of Mexico.

CANADA

UNITED STATES

Gulf of Mexico

PANAMA

Their flight speed averages 25 to 30 miles per hour. A hummingbird can dive at 60 miles per hour.

They feed by lapping rapidly from flowers and feeders with a tongue shaped like a "W."

A hummer can rotate each wing in a circle and is the only bird that can fly forward, backward, up, down, sideways, or just hang in the air.

WHERE TO FIND MORE ABOUT HUMMINGBIRDS

Websites:

Hummingbirds; www.hummingbirds.net

The Hummingbird Web site; hummingbirdworld.com/h/

Debbie's Tips for Attracting and Feeding Hummingbirds;
www.birdwatchers.com/debtips.html

How to Enjoy Hummingbirds; howtoenjoyhummingbirds.com

Flowers to Attract Hummingbirds;
landscaping.about.com/cs/forthebirds/a/hummingbirds.htm

Books:

Stokes Hummingbird Book: The Complete Guide to Attracting, Identifying, and Enjoying Hummingbirds, by Donald & Lillian Stokes. Boston: Little, Brown and Co., 1989. (ISBN 978-031681-715-8)

Creating a Hummingbird Garden, by Marcus Schneck. New York: Simon & Schuster, a Fireside Book, 1993. (ISBN 978-067189-245-6)

Attracting and Feeding Hummingbirds, by Sheri Williamson. Neptune City, NJ: TFH Publications, 2000. (ISBN 978-079383-580-5)